Lights

This book is dedicated to anyone who deals with depression or addiction.

It is never too late to change.

Never give up.

Contents

Part I: Mondays

Cold. I remember being cold as I walked out of my dorm and onto the street. Not just because of the mounds of snow beginning to pile up on the sidewalks or because some patch of ice on the ground caught me off guard and caused me to fall on my ass. It was because I got caught up doing calculus homework, and now I'm gonna be late, and the last time I was late to one of these things, it was a hassle at best. I just hoped that they would leave it alone this time. Late or early, it didn't matter; it was still gonna be a long night. I started to sprint down the street to save some time. When I got to the door, I checked my watch and saw that I actually got to the meeting five minutes early because of it. Despite my timeliness, however, most people had already walked in, and a couple had even begun to sit down. I've only been early once before, and in the time before the meeting starts, people from the previous meeting are usually cleaning up and having conversations all around the room. There aren't many people who come to either meeting, but from the look of it, people from both look pretty much the same: 30 to 40 years old, have two or more kids, greying or receding hair that they blame on their kids, and dressed in the clothes they probably wore to work that day. Everybody always looked so "business casual," which isn't a problem besides the fact that it always made me feel so out of place in my grey hoodie and sweatpants. I just turned 19, which made me the youngest person at every meeting, so it was never hard to pick me out. Especially when I was late. The last time I was late, I came in during some new woman's story. Much to her, and my surprise, there was a pack of cigarettes sticking out of my front pockets when I walked through the door. She took one look at me and then began hysterically crying and had to be taken outside to calm down. Apparently, her son had just died of lung cancer from smoking, and I must have reminded her of him. Needless to say, she didn't come back and that night, and I was the only thing we talked about. Usually, the regulars always welcomed me with a grimacing look because of that day. Thankfully, today everyone was already in a conversation or too preoccupied with twiddling their thumbs or watching the clock until we started to look at me.

I rarely interacted with anyone outside of my group. However, tonight, amongst all the heavy-set men who wandered about in their khaki pants and tucked-in button-down shirts, one stood out to me in particular. He was tall and skinny, and his thin wrists poked out from the sleeves of his overcompensating black coat. His hair was thin and, despite barely having any, was clearly gelled back in a futile attempt to hide his baldness. I must have stared at him for a while because when he turned to me, he gave me a snarky grin and started to walk over. His pace was startlingly fast, but it seemed like no one else saw him practically sprinting towards me. I looked away, pretending to take my seat, but as I was about to move, I felt a bony elbow crash into my ribcage. His fleece coat brushed against my arm, causing it to itch more and more with every tendril that pierced the upper layer of my skin. I looked up at his aged face. The skin on his right cheek had been bruised, forming blemishes under his eyes which were a deep shade of red. My body began to freeze as he leaned in close to my face; the weight of what was mainly his coat nearly knocked me over as he silently said to me,

"Don't worry, we're all infected here." His voice was rough, and his breath was hot. His stench was a concoction of liquor, cigarettes, and something I could only describe as shit.

"Wha—what!" I coughed then replied sternly, hoping he would stop using my chest as his personal armrest. I think he tried to respond with a laugh, but with all the phlegm in his throat, it sounded a lot more like he was choking than laughing.

"You know, I was just like you. I thought school was pointless, thought that cigs were just something to take the edge off. But then you start to get used to it. You start getting used to the control you have over how you feel. Then you start wanting something more. So, you go out, try different things, LSD, Meth, Heroin. You start playing with your mind. You start telling it, 'That's right, I decide how I'm gonna feel, I'm the boss here.' But really, you're just a passenger in your own life. Just a spectator. Watching it go by as you sit and grow older. And now, you've accepted it." He started to lean off me, and I was able to regain my footing. "You accepted that you're addicted, and soon enough, you'll learn that coming here just might be the best part of your goddamn week." I felt like telling him to go fuck himself for stating something so meaningless and for putting his entire body weight on me while he did it. But as I was working up my nerve, he began to pull in his coat and dart towards the door with the same speed he'd approached me with. That's when he turned around to look at me and said, "Or, you'll learn nothing here, and then kid, you'll be just like me." He showed me his broken smile, with chipped teeth whose cavities made them look more black than white, and whose gums were so inflamed that they appeared blood red. He then pulled out a cigarette and shut the door behind him.

I've been coming to these Drug Addicts Anonymous meetings consistently for a couple of weeks now. They met every Monday and Thursday, but I only went to the ones on Monday because I didn't want people to notice. The meetings are held in a basketball court inside of this gym, but on occasion, they're at people's houses when the gym is closed. I've been to every Monday meeting this month, but, then again, I also lied about being clean at every one of them. I tried to remember to stay away from drugs on Mondays and make sure I didn't smell like anything when I came. I was a lot more cautious ever since that day with the woman, but sometimes it was like they knew I had been doing drugs even if I didn't tell them. Even if they did know, it's not like anyone had the right to call me out. Most of them were really in the same boat as me. In the beginning, I think everyone legitimately wanted to quit and "cure" their addiction. However, over time, I think curing became a lot more like concealing. Being in college for a bit over a year had already begun to take its toll on me. I know it might sound stupid to someone who doesn't do drugs, but sometimes it really does feel like you need something to take the edge off. I started smoking regularly around the end of my first semester because it helped calm me down when I needed to study. Which, I mind you, was already a struggle. The few people who knew I smoked never failed to ridicule me for it. Not because they exactly had a problem with smoking, but because I was not trying the "healthier" alternative of vaping. I always told them, if I'm trying to relax, I'm better off using something that's going to last me a few minutes than sticking some USB flash drive in my mouth every two seconds. And carrying around a pack of cigs definitely beats having a 2-pound battery pack in my pocket all day. Smoking, for the most part, still kept me calm, but it sure as hell wasn't enough to keep me happy. I experimented with hard drugs before college, but when I got to school, I started using them somewhat infrequently. Mainly because it's much easier to buy cigarettes than it is to buy something like Heroine. Honestly, it wouldn't have really bothered me if people knew that I did drugs. I mean, most people in college do drugs. But the reason I couldn't have people know was because of my girlfriend, Amy. Both of her parents were addicts, and when we started dating, she was very adamant about her feelings on drugs and how we wouldn't be together if I started using them. We started dating early in our freshman year, and while she had some reasons to be suspicious, for the most part, I completely hid the fact that I did drugs from her. It's not like I was going to change her views, so I decided to just keep it to myself. I already planned on stopping after college anyways, so there was no reason to make her worry about me. Honestly, I kept most of my problems to myself because of her, but the more time we spent together, the harder it was getting to hide certain things. I guess I was scared that one day she'd notice if I had a lighter on me, or maybe I'd forget again and keep a cigarette packet sticking out of my front pocket for the world to see. All these little things really worked wonders for my anxiety, which maybe is what kept me in this loop where the more I tried to hide it, the worse my addiction got. I try to fight that aspect of myself, but maybe that's just who I am. Is that selfish? Sometimes I feel like I just use her to be happy even if I know that's not true. She really means the world to me. But, if she knew what I did, sometimes I feel like she wouldn't want to stay with me. Like maybe she'd be better off without me? I hate feeling like a burden but I can't shake the feeling that she'd be happier without me. Well, maybe not without me. Maybe just if I just wasn't me. I feel like she'd be better off if I was just like everybody else. Just a name and a face. No story, no baggage. Just a body, covering a hollow shell. Yep, just like everyone else.

Despite my initial encounter, the rest of the people who attend these meetings are pretty generic. Sandra is a 32-year-old housewife with two kids, Ally and John. She always begins the meetings by talking about how she's been clean for eight months and how amazing her life has been without drugs. We all know she's full of shit though. One day, she walked in with a black eye and bruises all around her right arm and cheek. She said she just "fell down the stairs," but, coincidentally enough, her husband also took away her credit card, and she's been clean ever since. She used to do really hard drugs, so it wouldn't surprise me in the least if she was hiding it from her husband. I'm pretty sure he's a lawyer or something that makes a lot of money. She mentioned it before, but I forget exactly what he does now. My guess is that when he found out what his wife was spending his money on, well, her bruises explain how he reacted. Jeffery's a 40-year-old man who only lives with his dog and works in construction. He's always late on-account of his car breaking down or his dog throwing up on his couch or something. He never really opened up about anything besides his smoking. Although, I guess that's all he can talk about if that's all he does. Andrew is 23, which makes him the second youngest person at the meetings. He used to talk a lot, but ever since his girlfriend broke up with him, he's been leaving early. I'm not sure how long they were together, but I assume it was a while because in addition to leaving early, he hasn't talked at any of the meetings since. We even used to hang out sometimes on the weekends, but lately he's been "busy," which I know is his excuse for sitting at home and getting high alone. At the meetings, he just sits there watching the clock until he feels ready to go home, which is usually halfway through Sandra's opening spiel. To be honest, he's another reason why I continue to come to these meetings, in addition to wanting to get better I mean. It's not like I'm checking up on him or anything, but sometimes I would come just to make sure he's still coming. As long as he was coming, maybe it meant he hadn't given up hope. If he didn't give up, then maybe it meant that it was still worth it for me to come. I think I see myself in him, which is why he really upsets me. That, and it's like no one except me cares about what he's going through. I understand people not caring about me or worrying if I talk or not, but Andrew used to be a pretty social guy. He liked making friends with all the people here, and he was the only person I could really relate to. Whenever I'd see him come to these meetings, socializing and doing well, I think it gave me a glimpse of hope for myself. Nowadays, people just skim over the fact that he only stays for the whole meeting once in a blue moon. He always looks like he hasn't showered in weeks and is on the brink of crying, holding his head down and saying nothing for the entire time he's here. I'd say something, but he wouldn't take my concern seriously because he still sees me as a kid. Regardless, it's the fact that nobody else will go talk to him when he's turning to leave that pissed me off. It's like everybody is so fucking blind, and these are the people who are meant to help. The truth that no one wants to admit is that nobody wants to help him because that would mean actually looking deeper. It would mean taking a few seconds out of their time to prioritize Andrew: a perfect stranger who everyone can see desperately needs somebody's help. Someone who's always screaming the loudest despite never making a sound. I guess I'm just as bad as them for not trying, but I just don't know what to do. Then there's John. Fucking John, who always has to be the last one to speak. Normally I wouldn't care either way, but this guy always holds up the meeting. He loves to go on and on about the most meaningless things. The first week was about his wife, then his hair, then his kids, then his house, then his car. I swear this guy and his fucking car! Last week, Sandra was telling us about how Caren, who's been coming to these meetings since forever, is now in the hospital with leukemia. Sandra was midway through her sentence when John had to jump right in, talking about how he thinks he should look for a new car because the suspension is giving out. He might as well have said, "Fuck Caren, I hope she dies from leukemia; the real problem is that my Honda's getting old." It's genocide for my brain cells whenever he opens his mouth, and of course, no one in the group has the spine to stop him, so he just babbles on about nonsense and then leaves scot-free. People like John make me want to stop coming to these meetings and just try going back to church. Hell, the people there go on endless tangents too, but at least I could catch up on some sleep if I'm in church.

The meetings are at night and go from 8 to 10. Every second took away a year from my lifespan. I don't have many good memories from these meetings, but the worst was the first meeting I went to. On my first day, I came half an hour late, so everyone glared at me when I walked in. I had to do that "Hi, my name is Allen, and I'm an addict" bullshit, and I couldn't get comfortable in the cold metal chairs. I was constantly moving around like an idiot, which doesn't look good if you're trying to keep a low profile in a room of literally 5 to 7 people. The time I was there was nothing short of torture. Everyone was naturally trying to get me to open up about why I was there, but what I hated more than that was everyone staring at me. When people stare at me, I feel like I'm physically suffocating. My skin feels hot, and I forget to take breaths between my words which makes me feel like I can't breathe. During that first meeting, I was so anxious that I almost lit a cigarette in the middle of the gym. It was Andrew who helped me out, he cut me off and started talking about something I forget now, but I thanked him for it afterward. I don't know if he meant to save me or if I was just stuttering so much that he thought I was finished speaking. Either way, it got everyone's attention off me, which allowed me a chance to breathe. He said it wasn't a problem when I thanked him after the meeting, and he offered to take me to the next one as long as I let him have one of my cigarettes. Without him, I definitely wouldn't have come back. The whole situation was probably what added to my feeling of being obligated to come as long as he came. I never really had to talk at any of these meetings after that day. Me and Andrew used to make subtle jokes to each other, but that ended when his girlfriend left him. It's not like anyone else cared if we talked or not. If anything, it just gave them more time to speak, which is really all they cared about.

I was still thinking about the guy from earlier, so by the time I got to my seat, we were already a couple of minutes into the meeting. I had to deal with everyone's grimacing looks even despite coming early. I saw some new faces when I looked around but, to be honest, it took me a while to distinguish them from the regulars. Sandra was taking, so I assumed I missed their introductions, which was fine by me because I always find them annoying as hell. I began to sit down, but as I looked around, I saw John's face as he cocked back a snarky remark.

"Seems like somebody took their time to take their seat." John's mistake was saying this in the middle of Sandra talking about getting her kitchen remodeled, which caused her to glare at him, almost in disbelief. Sure, he could cut her off when she's talking about someone who just got cancer, but butting in when she's talking about her kitchen? That was unforgivable.

"I'm sure Allen will try to be more punctual next time." She quickly snapped at John after taking a second to compose herself.

"Uh, yeah so—" Sandra cut me off.

"Gosh, I completely forgot what I was saying now. Thanks, guys."

Sandra didn't notice, but everyone gave a sigh of relief when she said that, knowing that the worst of the meeting was over. Sandra sat there for a minute while everyone was silent. She started to look around when her eyes finally fell on John.

"Well, John, you seemed to have a lot to say before. Care to take the floor." Despite being an almost criminally conceited person, Sandra making this kind of statement was pretty out of character. Recently she'd been trying to be more of a leader in the meetings, being nice and getting people involved and whatnot. John, of course, was no stranger to pettiness, however, and had a rebuttal of his own.

"You know, yeah, there is something I wanted to talk about. As most of you know already, I've been in the market for a new car recently." At the sound of this, Andrew began to get up from his chair and head towards the door. I saw his eyes sink towards the ground as he turned to grab his coat off the back of his seat. It was something about that sound, the one of him pushing back on the metal chair and having it scrape against the polished wooden floor. Something about that sound sparked a reaction in my body, and the next thing I knew, I joined Andrew in standing up.

"Hey, Andrew, why don't…" my voice drifted off into a whisper when I saw Andrew's eyes lock with mine. At that moment, it wasn't only the pressure of Andrew's stare but the feeling of everyone's eyes crawling over me that made it hard to breathe, let alone speak. I felt my knees buckle and my heart sink with embarrassment, all while Andrew's cold blank expression caused my body to shrink until I faded out of sight. I looked at him for a while. His stare, communicated a message as clear as if he had spoken it. It said, "Stop Allen. You can't help me. Let me go." When you feel a deep enough connection to someone, it comes to a point where looks alone start to become the primary form of communication. A passing glance could mean "See you at eight." A smile, "Run. Get help." A cold blank stare, "Walk away, and don't look back." I sat down after that stare. Andrew headed towards the door, and of course, everyone acted as if nothing happened. But then again, I guess nothing did. When the meeting was over, I stepped outside, and I saw something that made me feel like sprinting back in and asking John to remind me what dealerships he was looking at.

"OMG is that Allen Christan Jacobs." Stephanie Amber is arguably one of the most disgusting human beings I know. She's spoiled, arrogant, ignorant, and talkative as all hell. Her voice is an egotistical, ear-splitting shrill, that makes every meaningless word that comes out of her mouth, that much more painful to listen to. She'd be the female version of John if it wasn't for her platinum blonde hair, a stark contrast from John's dark brown. She said she was here to pick up her dad, so he must have been one of the new people I saw. Whenever I saw Stephanie, it was around campus or in my English class. She always made it apparent that she was talking to me by screaming my full name until I stop cowering in fear and address her. "OMG, why are you here?!" Stephine screamed and then gasped obnoxiously, "Have you been doing drugs?" What an idiot. I mean, I wouldn't expect her to know whether or not I did drugs, besides the fact that I was walking out of a fucking Drug Addicts Anonymous meeting. All she had to do was read the sign posted on the door to see why I was in there. Just the way she said it too. You could tell she really didn't care what the answer was, she was only talking to hear herself speak. Needless to say, I didn't answer the question, which I guess only made things worse. "OMG, you're totally a full-blown addict now, aren't you?" She let out a laugh so loud and obnoxious that I think people across the street noticed. Like, who laughs at that? What kind of person is that? It's not like I cared about what Stephanie thought, she doesn't really know Amy, plus an airhead like her would probably forget about our encounter by the time she got back into her car. Either way, it still pissed me off, and it was what she said after that which scared me. "Wow, I wonder what Taylor's gonna say seeing you here."

"What!" I looked behind Stephanie and the parasite crawling out of her bright pink Volkswagen was Taylor Fitzgerald. Taylor used to be what I guess you could call an old mutual friend between me and Amy. She's the one that introduced us to each other, but, apparently, her intention was never for us to get together. I heard from someone, who heard from someone else, that Taylor liked me at the time. Although, I don't think that assumption has much merit. She never made a move on me or anything, and she's a pretty forward person. If Taylor did like me, I'm sure that I would be the first person to know about it. Amy stopped hanging out with her after she learned about her prolific drug use. In turn, I stopped seeing her too. I can't deny that maybe I hung out with her once or twice just to kick back and smoke a blunt or two with her. But when Amy cracked down on her using drugs, she really blew everything out of proportion. Taylor knew that Amy could never know that I did any drugs, so I trusted the confidentiality between us. I began to ignore her because I didn't want to go behind Amy's back. I also thought that Amy would get suspicious about me doing drugs if I hung out with her, so keeping my distance seemed like the safest choice. I ghosted her for about a month, so it wouldn't have surprised me if she hated me. I knew that if she saw me here and started spreading rumors, Amy would see right through me.

"Hey Taylor, guess who it is." Stephanie pointed at me, and Taylor looked up slowly until she was looking directly at my stunned face. She looked at me up and down and gave a slight grin.

"Oh, hey Allen." Oh hey! Did she think I was stupid?! As if I didn't know what she was saying to herself. "Oh, hey Allen, what an excellent opportunity to ruin your life you have just given me. I can't wait for Amy to find out about this." Of course, I couldn't think of a way to respond. I tried to think of what to say, but when I opened my mouth, all that came out were awkward breaths in attempts to make words.

"Allen's a full-blown addict now Taylor, he even goes to the—" I cut Stephanie off quickly before she got me into any more trouble.

"No, I'm not," I replied sharply. "I'm just here to see a friend." My heart felt heavy as I began to feel sweat building up on my forehead and underneath my arms.

"Right, I'm sure," Stephanie said. Taylor knew I was lying too. It was in the way she narrowed her eyes and yet never broke her powerful gaze with me that told me so. It seemed like we had been standing there silent for hours. In the time we were looking at each other, Stephanie had already gone inside to get her dad. Taylor only looked at me with more and more intrigue. She was purposefully being silent and allowing me to speak. It was like in one of those old spy movies. I had already fallen into her trap, and now she was asking if I had any last words.

"Hey, um. You're not gonna—you know, right?" I sheepishly asked.

"Hmm," she began to smirk at me again, which made me instantly regret even opening my mouth. "Why shouldn't I tell her? After all, she is your girlfriend. I feel she deserves to know." I felt like I was one second from throwing her against the wall. The fear in my gut made my head hurt so much that I couldn't think about what to say. I thought about playing it off as a joke but couldn't muster the strength to fake a laugh.

"Taylor, please, you know how much this means to her." My voice was shaky. It sounded like I was on the verge of bursting into tears, because I was. I could feel them building up in my eyes as I pieced together how my life was going to fall apart.

"Gosh, chill out man. I won't say anything. I'm actually glad you're here. I wanted to tell you about a party on Wednesday. It's at Chris's place."

"Whose?"

"Ugh, you know nobody." She took out her phone and showed me the address. The party was in Manhattan, I recognized the address from flyers around the school that some frat guys were putting up.

"Oh, that party." I tried to say it in a way that let her know that I had no intention of going. She rolled her eyes at me and still persisted.

"Come on, you should come. These guys really know how to have fun." As she said that, Stephanie stepped out of the building with her dad and signaled Taylor to follow her. "Think about it, ok, Allen? Don't let Amy turn you into a total loser?" She lightly hit me on the arm to show that she was kidding, but my reflex told me to punch her in the mouth for saying that. Instead, I just curled my fists in my pocket and gave her a subtle nod. She got in the car and shut the door.

"Bye, Allen Christan Jacobs!" Stephanie screamed out her car window as she pulled out onto the road. God, I hate Mondays.

Part II: Winter and Her Nature is Cold

I woke up staring at my phone. All I could remember from last night was pacing around my room, waiting for a message from Amy. I don't know what it would've said, but all I knew was that if Taylor told her anything about what happened last night, whatever it was wouldn't have been good. It was 12:50 in the afternoon, so I think it was fair to say that I was in the clear. However, I still continued to stare at my phone, filled with unwarranted anxiety. Amy and I both don't have classes on Tuesdays, so we said we'd take the day to go out. We usually don't go out during the winter because she's sensitive to the cold. However, I was able to convince her to come with me to see a poem reading at a cafe nearby. I've never been to a poetry reading before, but I'm very familiar with the atmosphere of this coffee shop. Everything there seems slowed down. The dimmed lights paint the room an amber yellow, and the scene appears somewhat familiar even if you've never been there before. The second floor of the shop has a smoking section, so I would usually go up there just to relax. There, you could find people who'd prefer to just listen and sink into the woven fabric of the booths. You could hear every whisper, every side conversation about someone's day. I'd always eavesdrop and hear someone talking about how they love their new pet, or new house, or new car. It was always the same little things. Even though sometimes the talking annoyed me, the predictability of it all is what made it so great. Sitting on those couches and knowing everything that was going on. It made you feel like you're in a dream. You start feel like you can do anything, yet still, you choose to do nothing. You just sit there, and even though you feel like you're dreaming, you're awake. Everything you were seeing was real. So, you never had to wake up.

Amy said she'd be coming around 2, so I decided that it was probably a good time to take a shower and freshen up before she arrived. My roommate is a guy named Terrance. He has big curly brown hair and the kind of facial hair that makes you look like you're 30. It looked kind of like a shaggy goatee in the front, but it connected all the way to the back of his jaw on the bottom. Terrance is a nice enough guy, I guess, but somehow his clothes always ended up everywhere. Last week I saw his shirt was hanging off the lamp, and his pants were on top of the TV. Yesterday the floor was lined with his socks, and the bathroom had at least three pairs of his underwear in it. He said he was gonna "fold them up" but forgot, and then he laughed about it as if there was anything funny about his smelly socks all over the fucking room. I mean, it probably wasn't as big a deal as I'm making it out to be, but he did shit like that all the time. Maybe I got this from my mom. She was constantly cleaning the house. Partially because my dad lived like a pig, always leaving beers or cigarette buds around. Whenever I didn't pick up my shirt after a shower or something, she'd always have a conniption and give me a bunch of chores to do for the rest of the day. No doubt the mess here would have damn near killed her. Anyways, after taking a shower, getting dressed, and moving one of Terrance's shirts off the faucet to brush my teeth, Amy came. She was waiting on the other side of the door with the cutest fur coat. I always called it cute, but really, I thought it was sick. It was a black bubble coat with a huge hood, lined with light brown fur that fell over her eyes when she wore it. In the snow, it looked even better. When she stood outside, the white snow crystals began to melt all around the fur, creating a shimmering outline around the hood as if she was glowing.

"Hey Allen," she leaned in through the doorway to give me a big hug, most likely because it was a way to temporarily get out of the cold. "Are you ready to go?" Her cheeks were slightly pink from the cold, and her hair looked wet as if she too had rushed to take a shower just before she left. Her eyes were a beautiful hazel, whose reflection showed everything she was looking at in a brilliant light. I loved seeing the world through those eyes. The image reflecting back always seemed brighter than the actual scene, and it was accompanied by a beautiful light brown tint which made the reflection look like a dream.

"Yeah, let's go." I went to slip on my shoes and turned back towards the door. "See you later Terrance."

"See ya." He threw his hand up to wave goodbye and sent a sock flying across the room.

Amy and I started walking down the street towards the coffee shop. My dorm was at the edge of campus, so we were only about a 10-minute walk away. We never felt the need to make small talk. Making conversation was never my strong suit anyway, so not having to talk constantly is another reason why I enjoyed her company.

"Babe, aren't you excited? We haven't been on a date in so long!" Amy was always full of energy. I never understood how she could maintain it. Honestly, there was a lot about her that I didn't understand. She was always out volunteering, or tutoring, or babysitting. Literally, everything she did was for someone other than herself. Maybe her selflessness is what I loved so much about her.

Still, I don't think I'll never understand how she could keep up with it.

"Yeah, I'm excited, anything to hang out with my favorite girl." I turned and kissed her on the cheek, and she flashed her famous smile. Her face is filled with this light as her cheeks glow red. She shuts her eyes but still looks right at you with the biggest grin on her face. Every time, her face looks so happy that I almost question if it's real. It seems more like a face she had taken from a painting or a photograph. It had this magical spell to it too. It could cheer you up no matter what was happening. The best part of all was that it never lied to me. Even when we were fighting, she always had a way of looking at me and telling me exactly how she felt. Her face was always honest like that.

"Oh, is this it?" Amy pulled on my sleeve and pointed down the block. I turned and, ahead of me was the entrance to the Dusty Cafe. You could tell what building it was by the bright red door that had been renovated at least eight times and the same large crack on the top-right edge of the second stair, which had been there for as long as I remember. The reason why it's called the Dusty Cafe is because it's probably the only place in New York you can smoke and get some coffee that wasn't your house. The cafe was started by the owner's father back when smoking in these kinds of places was legal. When his dad died, the owner wanted to preserve his father's legacy in a way. Apparently, he was a pretty prolific smoker, so being able to smoke on the upper floor stayed. The owner's name is Jim, we talked about his dad when I asked him why this was known as the "smokers" coffee spot. He pretty much broke down the logistics of it all for me. His father bought the building and it was initially his house, until he renovated the first floor into a coffee shop. The second and third floors are technically still part of his house, which is why smoking was still allowed. You can only smoke in a little corner on the second floor, which is also the same floor that the poetry reading was on. I was already beginning to sweat thinking about how I was going to explain this to Amy. Naturally, the sign outlining where the smoking section was, was the first thing she saw when we walked in. When I told her where the poetry reading was, she was visibly not pleased. She finally agreed to going after I begged her to stay, and we made our way up the steps. Both floors were pretty much the same besides the addition of a stage and microphone on the second. Sometimes they had bands play here, and after hours the floor was set up back into the first level of the owner's house. For what it was, the cafe was actually really nice and successful. But, of course, Amy decided to ignore the calming decor and glare straight to the corner on the right. It was illuminated by the amber light of cigarettes and cloaked in a grey cloud of smoke.

"Ugh, how are they even allowed to smoke in here. I thought it was illegal." I thought I'd spare her the story and decided to ominously say that the owner had his ways. A statement which only heightened her resentment to the situation. Both of Amy's parents were drug addicts. They weren't abusive or anything, but Amy says they still hurt her from all the neglect. One time she summed it up for me and said that if they weren't high, it's because they were sleeping. Both of her parents were thrown into jail before her freshman year for possession, and her dad died there because he stole someone's cigarettes. Amy and her mom were devastated, but the pain really struck when Amy's mom had an overdose a couple of months after she got out.

Ever since then, her mom has been very "fragile," as Amy puts it. Needless to say, talking about any drugs to her is taboo. Even talking about her mom is a touchy subject. I don't think she really hates her parents, but at the same time, I guess I wouldn't blame her if she does. The thing is, she uses her experience with drugs to dictate her views on other people. I tried telling her how everyone who uses drugs isn't the same, but this is one topic I don't think I'll be able to change her mind on. After we picked the seat furthest from the smoking section, we began to look at the menu. "I swear this better be some awesome coffee, or the poetry better blow me the hell away, Allen."

"Don't worry, I swear it'll be worth it." I tried to crack a smile even though I knew that she was being completely serious. She always uses my name when she is being serious. We both ordered a coffee, and she got this avocado toast thing to come with it. I never really ate any of the food when I came here. I was always too preoccupied with smoking and never really felt hungry, so I couldn't tell her if anything was good or not.

"What, do you only get coffee when you come here?"

"No." I answered way too fucking fast. "I just, I'm never hungry, I guess you know." Thankfully my alibi here was that I'm basically skin and bone, so when I said that, she kind of looked at me up and down and then smirked. The first person who walked up to the stage to speak was a girl who looked like she was at most 18. She was Asian, a bit chubby, and had a round face that made her look really young.

"Hey, she's a freshman in my philosophy class. Her name's Ashley." Amy whispered to me and then began frantically waving from her seat until she caught Ashley's eye. It made her smile and give a soft but quick wave back before looking down at her paper. This made Amy smile which I thought was a pretty positive turn from where I thought the date was going.

"Hi, my name is Ashley Lee, and this poem is called beauty.

Beauty to me was once your smile, large and
gleaming
Beauty to me was you holding me tightly
Beauty to me was us together, dreaming
Beauty to me was knowing you'd sleep with me
nightly

Beauty to me was once seeing inside your mind
Beauty to me was your voice, sweet and soft
Beauty to me was always having your time
Beauty to me was us together getting lost

But now you are not here: my greatest fear
And your beauty can no longer grace my eyes
Now you, my beauty, have vanished, my dear

Now beauty is lost because you wouldn't try

Your face is gone, but our love is timeless

Now I must find beauty within the silence."

Amy began jumping up and down in her seat. She was smiling and clapping while the rest of the room was snapping and silently judging Amy for her sudden outburst of happiness. It made me smile though. Seeing her so happy was certainly a weight off my shoulders. Ashley was smiling too, although she turned away from Amy in embarrassment. She began stepping down when Amy snapped around in her seat and told me how much she liked the poem.

"You know, I bet you could be a good poet."

"Yeah, ok, Amy."

"Hey, I'm serious. You have that aura about you. It's very mysterious."

"Sounds kind of sexy."

"Oh, it's very sexy." She let out another joyful laugh. Next was a man in his mid 30's named Kyle. I know his name because I remember seeing him a couple of weeks ago. He wore the same burgundy get-up with his dark grey scarf and glasses, which probably had no prescription. I don't really remember him reading anything, but I do remember him going up to every girl that walked in to tell them that he was a poet. I don't really know what his deal is, but he seems like the kind of guy that would really get on my nerves. Usually, I just try to ignore him, but being that today I was here with Amy, I knew I was really in for it.

"Hello." He proceeded to take a long pause as if he was waiting for the applause in his head, telling him that what he wrote was the new Shakespeare, to stop. My eyes started drifting all around the room. I already felt his monologue coming.

"My name is Kyle Greyson, and much like the previous poet, my work is also one of remembrance. The action where we seclude our minds and hide in the past. In a way, it's all we know. The future has yet to come, and the present consists of but fleeting moments. But we can always return to the past. In its permanence, we can exist indefinitely. In the past, we can remain forever."

"Was that the poem?" Amy whispered over to me as the room began to snap. I couldn't help laughing a little until Kyle glared over in our direction, probably feeling like we were the only ones not appreciating his genius.

"My poem is Remembering the Fall." He said in a slow, quiet tone.

"Oh god, wake me up when it's over," I whispered to Amy, making her chuckle.

"I remember emotion as a mask to hide my face

I remember being numb, and it making us the same

I remember…"

I actually put my head down, intent on dozing off. But as I looked towards the smoking section, I saw a familiar face smiling at me. His name was Ryan. I met him through Andrew. I know he's a few years older than me but

I think he was still younger than Andrew. Honestly, he's a pretty chill guy once you get to know him, but at the same time, he's also a major dick. I don't know if he tries to be, but he always fucks with people when they don't want to be fucked with. Which, admittedly, can be really funny at times, but I know he'd probably get me in a lot of trouble if I struck up any conversation. I tried to look away and pretend like I didn't see him, but he kept on gesturing to me to come over, waving his cigarette in the air like a teen girl waving her phone flashlight at a fucking Harry Styles concert. All of this was happening right behind Amy. I was surprised that she didn't question the amount of sweat profusely running down my face as I tried to think of what to do. I began to twist my toes and pick at my nail with my finger. It's something I always did when I was anxious. Amy knew this, of course, so I threw my hands into my pockets and sat there silently until she began to stand up from her seat.

"Hey, I'm going to the bathroom. I'll be right back."

I nodded quickly and tried to mumble a quick "mhmm" of assurance. All I could get out was an awkward low tone, which caused her to giggle as she walked straight towards the bathrooms. I quickly got up from my chair when I saw she was leaving and walked towards Ryan.

"Hey, if it isn't the kid himself!" Ryan greeted me loudly, alerting the people at the tables around him. I already knew Kyle was probably trying to burn a hole in the back of my head with his eyes, but I had already tuned him out a while ago. Before I was able to talk, I glanced over at Ryan's left hand. The cigarette he held was half-smoked, and I almost instinctively went to take it before I stopped myself and refocused.

"Ryan, I can't talk right now. I'm with my girlfriend Amy, and she really doesn't like this kind of stuff, so you have to stop?"

"Kinda stuff?" He saw my eyes and noticed I was talking about his cigarette. "You mean smoking? What she doesn't know you smoke?"

"No, she doesn't, so maybe we can talk a different tim—"

"Allen?" I heard Amy's voice in a whisper right behind me as I fought the urge to whip around in a cold sweat.

"Amy." I tried to mirror her hushed tone to not annoy anyone else sitting by Ryan. Probably the only person concerned with us was Kyle. "I thought you said you had to go to the bathroom?"

"I did, but there was a bit of a line. Why are you—"

"He just came to talk to me." Ryan put out his cigarette, got up from the table, and walked towards Amy. "Hi, my name's Ryan." He stuck out his hand, but I saw Amy was already about to start reeling from the smell of the smoke.

"It's the smell, Ryan."

"What?"

"She's a bit allergic to the smoke." I saw Amy glaring at me in my peripherals, probably from telling such a stupid lie. I also think it was her growing suspicion that caused her aggravated reaction.

"Allergic, must be a little dangerous coming here then, right?" He chuckled at his joke while Amy kept the stern look on her face.

"I'm not allergic. I just really hate the smell."

"Oh, I see. Well then, how do you hang around this guy all day, huh?" He slapped me on the shoulder, but he might as well have smacked me in the face. I looked over to Amy first to see her angry glare turn into a more confused look, staring right up at me. It was then when I was going to whip around and punch Ryan in the face when I felt his arm start to rest on my shoulder. "I'm kidding, I'm kidding. We both know your smell just comes from a lack of showers buddy." His unapologetic laughter caused me to put my hand back in my pocket and nervously pick at my nail with my finger. I use my other hand to try and create some distance between myself and Ryan.

"We were just pushing off, but maybe I can properly introduce you guys another day, alright?" He sensed I was starting to get annoyed, so he smirked at me and took his arm off my shoulder. He began to turn around and walk back to his seat, all the while saying nothing and waving goodbye. I tried to quickly usher Amy out of the room as I turned around. Kyle was now entirely focused on me as he continued reading his poem. As Amy and I were making our way out of the room, I could see more people starting to look at us. Every glaring pair of eyes just made me move faster until I began pulling Amy out of the cafe. When we got outside, Amy stopped immediately and turned around to look at me.

"What was that all about?" Her face was turning scarlet red, and her arms were folded across her chest as she demanded an answer.

"He's just an old friend. I haven't talked to him in a while." I felt like I needed to be cautious about everything I was saying. I knew that she'd know whether or not I was lying. I'm a terrible liar when it comes to Amy. My hands start to sweat, so I always put them in my pockets. I can never stop stuttering, and I always try my best not to look her in the eyes.

"What was he was talking about when he mentioned how you smell? And why did you say that I was allergic?"

"I don't know Amy. I think he was just—"

"Have you been smoking Allen?" I knew now that she was in a controlled rage because she was using my name.

"No, Amy, come on. I was. It wasn't. It was a while ago okay. We just used to hang out and—"

"And you just smoked and got high, right?"

"Amy, no, he's just a guy I used to know." I felt the inside of my pockets begin to feel wet. The sweat from my palms was beginning to mix with the blood that came from me picking at my fingernail. I didn't make eye contact with her, but I could assume what the aggravated look on her face would be like. Probably the pink scrunched-up face she made whenever she was talking about her parents.

"Allen, are you?" I looked up for a moment when her voice went quiet. She was staring at the ground. "Allen, why are you lying to me?" I could feel the tears in my eyes start to build up. I tried to look up with every ounce of strength I had, but my eyes were glued to the ground. I bit my lip until I felt it bleed. I tried to reach out and hug her, but my arms felt too weak to move. All I could do was stare down at the concrete as I tried to think of a good lie or anything that could get me out of the situation. That's when I raised my hand to my eyes to not let her their scarlet hue as I looked up to face her.

"Can we please talk about this later?" I could smell the blood coming out my thumb as I brought my hand to my face. The sting of my eyelashes rubbing against the exposed flesh is what caused me to give up on uttering any more words as I stood in silence. Amy let out a large, exhausted breath.

"Alright, Allen." As she turned to walk away, I finally removed my hand from my eyes to look at her. I reached out to hold her hand, but as she turned around, my hand retreated back into my pocket. She saw the tears now clearly flowing down from my eyes. "I'm gonna go back in a bit. I just want to be alone right now. We can talk about this some other time."

"Alright." My first instinct was to lean in and give her a hug, but as my body moved forward, she had already begun to walk away. She walked in the opposite direction of our campus, and, in what felt like a matter of moments, made it out of my sight. I started turning around to go back to my dorm, but as my eyes began to cross the cafe, I saw Ryan standing in the doorway. He had one foot on the top stair and the other moving towards the crack, causing him to tumble as he made his way out. I didn't have the strength to scold him, but he was visibly saddened when he looked at me. I had no doubt that he'd been smoking all day, but my eyes were now redder than his due to the tears. He placed his hand on my shoulder and handed me a lit cigarette with the other. I took it out of his hand and then began to slowly take in every amount of smoke I could fit into my lungs. He took out a new cigarette and lit it for himself as he turned me around, and we began walking towards campus. Only when we had made it a block down did he utter,

"Sorry bout' that, Allen." To which I replied with a large cloud of smoke and a quiet,

"It's alright." Ryan and I walked around for a while before I went back to my dorm. That night I barely slept at all. When I got back, I did nothing but stare at the ceiling for what felt like hours on end. When my knees finally got tired, I threw myself into bed, trying my hardest not to cry as I slowly faded into unconsciousness.

Part III: Lights

When I wake up, I usually start my day by staring at my dry and unkempt black hair in the bathroom mirror. Sometimes I'd even grab one of Terrance's shirts he left lying about and try to wipe the oiliness off of my face until I decide to take a shower. I don't usually start my day by staring at my phone, waiting for a text from Amy talking about how I betrayed her trust and how we're going to have to break up. Although, recently it seems like that is becoming my new routine. It was Wednesday, and I pretty much went straight to my dorm after my morning classes. Whenever I wasn't eating or sleeping, I was glued to my phone. I just sat there, scrolling through Amy's past messages and screaming at myself for being such an idiot. I spent most of the day drafting an apology, but I never could send anything. Honestly, it didn't even feel right texting her. If she wanted to talk, she would have reached out. Who was I to send her something and expect her to read it? As if my words even mattered to her anymore. This continued for the whole afternoon until I heard Terrance say that he was leaving to go to a party. It was a little while until I connected the dots and figured out that his party was probably the same one Taylor was talking about on Monday. I hated doing it, but I started to consider going. If anything, it could at the very least be a way of getting yesterday off my mind. I didn't really like frat parties. In fact, I hated them. I wouldn't exactly call myself a fan of dancing, or partying, or drinking. Loud music and hundreds of people sweating on each other in the middle of some rich kid's parent's apartment never really correlated to "fun" in my mind either. But I knew these frat guys usually had the good stuff at their parties, and I knew the guy who was dealing. He and I were on good terms, so I figured I could probably get whatever he was selling cheaper than if I bought it online. I had already blown through most of my college cash, and I smoked a whole three packs just sitting in my room. I hadn't smoked this much in a long time. When I stood up, I felt weak and had to move slowly to get around. I hadn't done any hard drugs in a while either, but I felt like it would really help numb me out. It was already 10, and Amy still hadn't texted me, so I figured she was probably asleep. I put on some jeans and a black dress shirt that I had underneath a pile of textbooks and one of Terrance's socks and caught a ride to the upper east side of Manhattan. On my way to the party, Amy finally texted me, asking what I was doing. There was no way I could have mustered the strength to respond and tell her I was headed to a party. I was also already half an hour out and didn't feel like turning around, so I put my phone on do not disturb, and looked out the window as I tried to relax.

The city is so beautiful at night. I always look at it as its own world. Like the second version of Earth that humanity created. Except, in this manmade world, we traded the stars for led lights and the trees for buildings and stores. The dirt paths became concrete sidewalks and tar-filled roads. The animals were miles and miles of backed-up traffic. Each car horn roaring was like a wolf howling, as their sound permeated throughout the city and lasted throughout the night. In the city, humans become like insects. Like bees or ants, we all follow our separate paths but still stay so closely connected when we return to our tall glass hives and cold brick colonies. The world can seem so small at times. Every minute detail can seem to be personally catered to your life. But in the city, everything is so large. It makes all the people seem small and insignificant. The big-time lawyer becomes indistinguishable from the single working mother of three. The homeless look about as unique as the bits of trash on the street everyone walks past and ignores. People just continue walking along the same narrow path, sandwiched between the blinding light from cars on the road and the darkness of the silent buildings. Everything you are begins to fade away here. You become so small that you disappear. You disappear, and nobody notices.

It started raining by the time I got inside the hotel. The party was at one of the fraternity guy's parent's luxury apartments at the top of a new building. There are only 15 floors, but with the time it takes for the elevator to come down, you'd think there were 500. I debated just taking the stairs, but it still felt hard to move. If I walked up all those flights of stairs, I probably would have died before I made it to the party. Plus, I just avoided getting wet from the rain outside, so I didn't want to get there and be drenched in sweat instead. The elevator eventually came, and I took it straight up to the fifteenth floor. When I got into the room, I was hit with a thick cloud of smoke from somebody's blunt, which told me I was in the right place. The music was so loud that the ground started shaking. There were so many people pushing you around that walking seemed to become pointless. The "dance floor" was literally the entire first floor of the apartment. If you weren't tall, your best bet to not get elbowed in the face would have probably been to curl up in a ball and run the risk of being picked up and tossed around. Off to the right, I saw my old friend Sam dealing out of one of the bathrooms. On the street, he would just offer stuff like weed. It was parties like these where he sold Ketamine, LSD, Ecstasy, things like that. Getting in line to talk with him was like getting in line to meet the pope. There were about 40 people ahead of me, all waiting for the same thing. Five minutes later, the number of people behind me matched the number of people in front, and that's not including the people who came tumbling off the dancefloor, colliding into everyone around them. The girl in front of me could have been topless for all I knew. All I could see of her was the bareness of her back, and the guy behind me was a 6'7 beast who acted like I was trying to hold up the line. Every time I stopped moving, he pushed me forward, and the four people ahead of us moved with me. It was about 20 minutes till the girl in front of me ran off with a bag of pills. I saw Sam crouched up on the toilet. "Hey, Sam. How's it been?" I asked him while laughing at how regal he looked, like a king atop his porcelain throne. Sam was a blonde guy who looked way too old to be at a college party. He was only 26, but his beard made him look like he was ten years older, and the guy's voice added about five more years on top of that. Sam had made a sort of monopoly on drug dealing by selling at these parties. He hasn't gotten caught yet and now does pretty much whatever he wants. He even brings this high school kid named Daniel, who he calls his brother, to these things. Dan's not actually his brother, but somehow, they know each other, and Sam seems to care a lot about him. I talk to Sam outside of school every so often. He tells me about all the parties he goes to and the various things he does to sell drugs. I've even talked to Dan on occasion. He isn't really a nuisance, like I assume a sixteen-year-old to be, though we never really spoke one on one. I'd see him occasionally whenever I went to visit Sam. By Sam's account, Dan is pretty much a genius. He's only 16, and he's already graduating high school. Sam uses him to do all the accounting for his little drug empire. He keeps track of the supply, the profit and helps him coordinate where he's gonna sell. They're kind of like business partners in a sense, but at the same time, I still kind of feel bad for him. I don't think that a kid should be living that kind of life. But, then again, I still buy from them, so who am I to talk.

"Hey, if it isn't my favorite junkie, Allen. How have you been?" The smell of the bathroom was undoubtedly better than the stench of sweat from the hundreds of people outside. Sam always called me his "favorite junkie," but I think it was just to taunt me more than anything else. All the people that knew I do drugs knew I tried to hide it. Sam liked teasing me about it, and pretending like I'm the biggest addict he knew.

"Hey, Sam. I've been good." I didn't feel the need to tell him about all the things that Amy and I were going through. It was probably better that he didn't know anyways.

"So, what do you want?"

"You got any PCP?"

"Shit Allen. Did something happen?" It wasn't too unusual for someone to buy PCP from Sam. Hell, I'm sure he sold much worse to many other people. But that was the thing about Sam; he was always pretty weird with how he handled drugs. He'd only sell you something that can really hurt you if he knew you enough to like you. But at the same time, he also didn't like it when people bought anything too hardcore from him if he considered them a friend. He never refused to sell to someone, but he'd always make sure you knew that he didn't want you buying whatever it was. He was strange like that, which I guess is why he had Dan running the business side of things.

"I'm fine Sam, I'm just feeling in the mood today, I guess. You know?" Sam let out a large sigh.

"No, I don't know. Man, I never know with you. I feel like every time I see you, you're looking better but acting worse." He was angrier than how I thought he'd be. I haven't bought anything like this in a while, so I don't know why he was overreacting. Plus, it wasn't like he was going to refuse to sell it to me. Not with the mile of crackheads behind me, all coming to buy things far worse than what I was buying. I liked Sam, but sometimes he can be so dreadfully ordinary. Just putting up a facade, just a show to defend his already weak set of morals. Just lying to keep up appearances like everybody else. God, why can't people just be honest with how they feel. It's always just a charade, just dancing around all the difficult things because we're so scared. It's so stupid. It's so... so pathetic. I zoned out for a minute while standing there. I think smoking too much was starting to mess with my head. When I snapped back to reality, I saw Sam as he searched around. He reached in his duffle bag behind the toilet and grabbed a small plastic bag with the drugs. "Alright, man. Just be careful." He handed me the bag and then leaned back against the toilet. I took out my wallet, but he and I both saw that I only had a couple of fives. "Just give me what you got." He said with an agitated look on his face after glancing at the bills I had and then at the growing line behind me. It took me a minute to respond. First, I had to comprehend what he was saying over the booming music, and then I had to think about what to say.

"Thanks, man. I promise I'll make it up to—" Sam cut me off.

"I already gave you the discount Allen. Don't make promises you can't keep." He said this with an even angrier tone as he snatched the money out of my wallet. Inside the bag was everything except the syringe and a spoon which he handed me separately. I tried asking if I could stay in the bathroom to take the shot, but now the giant who was behind me was breathing down my neck. The people behind him also seemed pretty antsy, so I decided to just walk away. I had to cut through the war zone of a dance floor to get some water from the kitchen. I put the syringe in my pocket, but every time someone slammed into me, it stabbed me in the thigh, so I decided to just hold it in my hand. It worked as a deterrent for people slamming into me, but it also made me look like a maniac, so I tried to keep my head down as I walked. I took a stop at a table to catch my breath and fill a solo cup with some beer. After I was done drinking, some jackass named Troy from my calculus class saw me fumbling my way to the sink, syringe still in hand.

"Yeah, Allen!" He obnoxiously screamed as he started clapping. People on the outskirts of the dancefloor began to turn around, only to see the uneventful scene of me pouring water from the sink into my cup. I hate it when people stare at me. It's like I can feel their eyes all over me. Suffocating me until my lifeless body was no longer of interest. No one really looked at me for a long time. They more so only turned around for a second and then faced back towards the dance floor when they couldn't find the reason why Troy was clapping. Just as I was finishing filling my cup with water, I felt a light tap on my left shoulder.

"Hey, Allen." I stopped the water and turned around to see Taylor's face. She looked pretty generic, aside from her necklace, which had gold a star-shaped pendant. It was surprisingly bright, even with the lights being off in the apartment. "Glad to see you could make it to the party."

"Hey, Taylor." I tried to limit the number of words I was saying. Partially because I already felt a bit tipsy from the beer. I also wanted to run off and take the shot before anyone else saw me. Taylor glanced at my hand with the syringe and let out a small chuckle.

"Wow, it looks like Stephanie was right about you. You are a complete addict now, huh?" I began to put the syringe in my pocket, but it collided with the spoon, and I stabbed myself again. I decided to keep holding onto it and gave her a forced smile as I tried to move past her. I pushed her out of the way with the hand holding my cup slowly so that I didn't spill anything. I was about to leave when she grabbed me and moved my hand away from her arm and onto her left breast.

"How about you come with me upstairs? I have a room waiting for us." I took one look at Taylor and couldn't help but laughing.

"Sorry, not that drunk," I replied coldly. I moved my hand away, this time with more force. I spilled a good bit of the water all over her outfit, something that made both of us angry. She looked down at her shirt, and I thought she was about to hit me. But then her face of anger and disgust quickly turned into a smile as she looked behind me and walked away.

"Suit yourself." She added as she disappeared into the crowd of people dancing and jumping around to the music.

"Stupid bitch." I quickly said underneath my breath.

"Allen."

Amy's voice was a gunshot, only I heard amongst the sound of blaring music and screams. I snapped around to see her so fast that everything in my cup had spilled out onto the floor. I gripped the syringe so hard I could feel the plastic bend as it was being warped by my hand. My eyes flooded with tears as I saw her face. It wasn't long before Amy's cheeks were blood red and wet with tears. "Amy, what are you—why are you here?"

"Taylor told me you were going to be here. She said you didn't tell me because you were afraid—what are you?" She glanced at the syringe in my hands and started choking on her words as she began to break down crying. More and more people began turning around, now stopping to stare at the dramatic scene behind them. My body was cold with sweat, but my head felt like it was on fire. For a moment, I was paralyzed. I didn't know if I should run upstairs, throw away the syringe, or curl into a ball, hoping that everyone would stop looking at me so I could collect my thoughts. It was after a moment that felt like a lifetime when I decided to speak.

"I—I'm sorry. I'm sorry! I'm so sorry, Amy!" I felt like Amy was trying to speak, but every time she opened her mouth, all I heard was the sound of her choking on tears. The louder she cried, the louder I screamed my apology until I felt like I was about to rip my vocal cords and drop dead on the floor. I turned my head and looked where I could run to on the other side of the wall of flesh in front of me. I saw that no one was on the balcony and thought that it was probably on account of the rain. I made a dash towards it, hoping to get some fresh air. Everyone looking at me moved out of the way as I raced past them. I brandished the syringe like a weapon now. I held it like a sword, armed to defend myself against the army of eyes that penetrated my head and seeped into my mind. I felt Amy's hand on my shirt, trying to grab onto me. She moved up and grabbed my arm, but when I turned around to move her, I realized I had cut her with the syringe.

I heard Amy cry out in pain. I was frozen for a second until I saw everyone's eyes facing me. I kept running until I was at the door of the balcony. There was tape around the handle, but I ripped it off and quickly stepped outside. By the time I understood what was happening, I immediately turned around to see if Amy was ok. She was grabbing her palm, violently sobbing as her blood dripped down her arm and onto the floor. After I saw her, Amy continued to chase after me for a few steps. She then began to slow down and sway back and forth. Her legs wobbled around, unsure if they really wanted her to move towards me. Her body pondered that question for a while until she finally stopped and took a step back. I was still holding the syringe, droplets of her blood on the point washed away in the ruthless pouring rain. I quaked in fear, crying on the balcony. Her body continued to make slight motions towards me as she debated going after me. I looked around, and now everyone was watching me. The sound of the music seemed to cut off, and all I could hear were the defending screams of Amy as I looked at her bloodied hand. Her face was now burning red and drenched with tears as snot ran down from her nose. She had made one last step towards me before her knees collapsed onto the ground. I began to walk backward as I grabbed my head. This was all my fault. Why did I come? Why couldn't I stop? I should have just turned back. I should have talked to her. Why was I here? Why wasn't she enough? My thoughts ran rampant through my head, the entire room went dark, and all I could see was Amy kneeling on the ground. I blinked hard to dissipate the tears from my eyes, but every time I opened them, the sight of Amy came closer and closer, and my thoughts grew louder and louder. I'm sorry Amy, please don't be mad, I didn't mean to, I never wanted this to happen, I should have just told you the truth, I swear I didn't mean to lie to you. Amy, I love you. I love you so much, and I'm sorry, I'm so—.

I blinked hard once again, but when I opened my eyes, the image of Amy disappeared. The railing I was leaning on must have been broken because when I looked to my right, there was a piece of tape attached to it. It was ripped and I saw the other half attached to the other railings that now were above me. I was falling. The city's bright lights flared around me, engulfing me into their flame. The rain had turned to snow, and it felt sharp as it rushed against my skin. It felt like it was cutting me into tiny particles, destroying me until soon I would become one with the air. Am I falling? Am I going to die? These questions were the only things on my mind until I started to try and imagine Amy. I imagined her reaching over the balcony, grabbing me before I fell too far out of her reach.

I attempted to see myself in the glass exterior of the apartment building. I glanced over but only saw a silhouette of my body reflected back at me in the apartment's black mirror. I felt my tears being lifted off of my cheeks and out of my eyes. As my vision cleared, I saw the crowd of people and miles of cars stuck in traffic below me. All lined up perfectly as if it was a picture. As if it was an image from a dream. When I turned to look back up, I thought I saw Amy's face leaning over the terrace. It was then when I felt like all the lights in the city had gone out. The world around me was dark. All that was left was a faint pink dot amongst a growing sea of black. Like the last beautiful star, amongst a dark, endless sky.

Made in the USA
Monee, IL
22 August 2021